Size 0

THE OPPORTUNITY

Size 0

D. M. PAIGE

darby creek

MINNEAPOLIS

Text copyright © 2013 by Lerner Publishing Group, Inc.

Darby Creek
A division of Lerner Publishing Group, Inc.
241 First Avenue North
Minneapolis, MN 55401 U.S.A.

Website address: www.lernerbooks.com

Cover and interior photographs © iStockphoto.com/Julie Weiss (girl);
© iStockphoto.com/Jordan McCullough (title texture).

Main body text set in Janson Text LT Std 12/17.
Typeface provided by Linotype AG.

Library of Congress Cataloging-in-Publication Data

Paige, Danielle.
    Size 0 / by D. M. Paige.
        pages   cm. — (The opportunity)
    Summary: "It's been one student's dream to work in fashion, but her internship with a trendy LA clothing company leaves her with reservations about how models are treated and how fashion affects body images"—Provided by publisher.
        ISBN 978–1–4677–1372–6 (lib. bdg. : alk. paper)
        ISBN 978–1–4677–1676–5 (eBook)
        [1. Fashion—Fiction. 2. Models (Persons)—Fiction. 3. Body image—Fiction. 4. Internship programs—Fiction. 5. African Americans—Fiction.]
    I. Title. II. Title: Size zero.
    PZ7.P154Si 2013
    [Fic]—dc23   2013006523

Manufactured in the United States of America
1 – SB – 7/15/13

In order to succeed, your desire for success should be greater than your fear of failure.

—Bill Cosby

PROLOGUE

Dear Ms. Roberts,

I am Harmon Holt. Yes, that Harmon Holt. And I am pleased to welcome you into the Holt Internship Program.

I am investing in the future. Every year, I select ten students who best exemplify the Holt legacy. Allow me to recognize your talent, your ambition, and your heart. You, Thea Roberts, are one of the ten.

If you accept, you will be spending the summer interning with one of the world's most talented designers, Lorelei Roy, at her studio in Los Angeles. All expenses will be covered by the Holt Foundation.

It may be hard for you to see this now, but the distance between the two of us is measured only in hard work and an opportunity. I am giving you the opportunity. The rest is up to you.

Good luck,
Harmon Holt

ONE

"You know those moments that can change your life? This is that moment, Thea Roberts."

Ms. Hampton, my guidance counselor, always spoke like the inside of a Hallmark card. But this was over the top even for her.

Her office was wallpapered with inspirational posters: "Hang in There," "You Can Do It," and "It Gets Better." The "Hang in There" poster was faded and its corners were all bent and it actually had a picture of a kitten hanging on a tree.

I looked at Ms. Hampton with a mixture of curiosity and confusion. I had never been called into the guidance counselor's office for an un-scheduled visit. I didn't get in trouble. Not ever. But judging by the too-wide smile on her face, that wasn't the issue.

Ms. Hampton clapped her hands together and let out a little cheerleader squeal. Then she handed me a blue envelope.

The last time someone handed me some-thing that changed my life, I was six. My gram had given me a sewing needle and thread. "Buy a girl a dress, she wears it for a season. Teach a girl to sew, she's clothed for a lifetime," she'd said.

At the time, I hated that Gram wouldn't buy me a new pair of jeans, the kind that everyone else was wearing. But once I learned how to use that little needle, it became my new best friend. I'd been sewing ever since. First, I copied what my friends were wearing. But later, I was mak-ing one-of-a-kind clothes that other kids actu-ally wanted to copy.

I turned the envelope over in my hands. It was light as a feather.

One little piece of paper can't change my life, I thought.

But I ripped open the envelope, unfolded the matching blue paper, and started to read.

My eyes scanned the page. Twice.

And I am pleased to welcome you into the Holt Internship Program . . .

Lorelei Roy . . .

All expenses . . .

"Lorelei Roy is my favorite designer!" I said. "How did this . . . ? There must be some mistake . . . I didn't even apply."

I looked from the fancy embossed stationery to Ms. Hampton's smiling face.

"There hasn't been a mistake," she said with a certainty that I didn't share.

TWO

Harmon Holt, like the other donors to our school, had always stayed as far away from our campus as the stars were from Earth. Rich people donated things like the new "healthy" vending machines in the cafeteria or the new band equipment or the new paint supplies. But donors didn't give once-in-a-lifetime opportunities. Or did they?

"You have been selected for a very prestigious internship," Ms. Hampton said.

"I don't understand. I didn't apply," I said, rereading the words.

Harmon Holt. As in Holt Entertainment. Holt Airlines. Holt Enterprises.

The Holt logo, two intertwined *H*'s, was everywhere from the credits on movies to the labels on clothes to the liner notes of hit albums.

There was even a mention of him in my econ book. But Harmon Holt was a name and not a face. He stayed behind the scenes, rarely making public appearances. So getting a personal letter from him was like getting a personal letter from my favorite member of my favorite boy band. And yet, there it was, a letter from a billionaire addressed to me.

I was waiting for the catch. People don't just hand you anything out of the blue. Not for free. At least, not once in my sixteen years.

"Harmon Holt? *The* Harmon Holt? But how?"

"You know, Mr. Holt is one of the school's biggest donors . . ." Ms. Hampton said.

I looked out the window. The one thing Holt couldn't change was the view. The school faced a string of ugly, empty, old buildings. Clinton High had been cleaned up, but that made its surroundings seem that much worse.

"Mr. Holt requests recommendations from me, the principal, and your teachers," Ms. Hampton continued. "When his assistant mentioned that there would be an opportunity in fashion this year, you were the only choice. Mrs. White made copies of your portfolio. I sent him footage of last year's fashion show."

Mrs. White was my favorite teacher. She gave me extras studio time and helped me with my fashion illustrations after school. The school's fashion show was on YouTube, but it had only got five hundred hits. One for every student at Clinton. It was so weird thinking of Harmon Holt watching my show. And picking me.

"You know, you could be a model yourself," Ms. Hampton said as she returned from finding a permission slip for me to give to Gram.

I had heard that sentence dozens of times before, but it was almost always followed by a pause. A pause that usually meant, if only I were thinner. I might have been five feet nine and blessed with my gram's pimple-free chocolate skin. But I wasn't skinny like those girls in magazines and on runways.

"Yeah. All I'd have to do is stop eating," I said.

Ms. Hampton's face fell. "I'm sorry, I didn't mean to . . ."

"Don't worry about it. Who wants to be a walking hanger for clothes when I can design them?"

Ms. Hampton's smile returned. She looked like she was considering writing down what I said and adding it to her poster wall.

"You leave a week from Friday."

I looked at Ms. Hampton's posters again. Clinton High was a school for dreams and dreamers. Or at least that's what was written on the plaque outside the school. But I had never dreamed this big. Los Angeles! Lorelei Roy! I hadn't ever even been out of DC, let alone to Los Angeles. This was really happening!

THREE

"Earth to Thea."

My BFF Bonnie demanded my attention, twirling one of her superlong locks with her finger.

I was still getting used to the hair. Bon had gone Beyoncé blonde last month. The blonde hair complimented her caramel skin and made her look like the star that she was destined to be. I wasn't jealous. I liked my own brown hair, the way it hung in waves down my shoulders. Bon wanted me to go blonde with her so we could be twins. But we could never actually be twins. At five feet one, she was like eight inches shorter and about thirty pounds thinner.

"Earth to Thea," she repeated.

We were sitting at our table at lunch. I was already in LA in my head, in a fashion showroom. Bonnie knew something was up. She had been my best friend since first grade, when she offered me a piece of Bubblicious kiwi strawberry gum. Bonnie was always giving me things: clothes she didn't want anymore that I could make over into something new and advice about boys, which I desperately needed.

"Spill it," she demanded before taking a gulp of her chocolate milk.

Looking around the cafeteria, I could feel the end of the school year in the air. We were all winding down. Yearbooks had been given out on Monday, another Holt perk. No one had to buy them this year. And our usual crew of theater geeks and art kids was all over the cafeteria, everyone signing one another's yearbooks. Some people were used to saying good-bye. But Bonnie and I saw each other every day. We had since we were five. If I went to Los Angeles, it would be the first time we'd been apart in forever.

The words came out in a rush.

After I'd told her everything, I worried that I was somehow letting her down—leaving her behind. Bonnie had things she wanted to do too. She was going to be an actress. But we were supposed to spend our summer together. Working at the local froyo shop to save money. Or getting jobs together at the mall.

But Bonnie didn't look disappointed. She looked thrilled. She hugged me, punching the lunch tray out of the way and squeezing me tight.

"You know what this means," she said over my shoulder.

"What?" I asked, trying to avoid a mouthful of blonde hair.

"You need to sew a whole new work wardrobe."

"But what about our summer?" I asked, breaking the hug and studying her pretty face.

Bon and I looked over at Dom at the exact same time. Dom was currently in the corner of the cafeteria, surrounded by a gaggle of girls.

They held their yearbooks for him to sign like he was someone famous.

Bonnie and I shared everything. Our secrets. Our clothes. And our crush on Domino James—the hottest guy in school, who happened to be one of our best friends. He hadn't shown the least bit of interest in either of us, though. Not in the crush kind of way.

Dom was an artist like me. But he was fearless like Bon. This summer was supposed to be the summer things were different. The summer Dom noticed one of us. I figured it would be Bonnie. I figured that it was already Bonnie and that Dom was being nice to me because he liked her so much.

Bonnie was going to be an actress. She already starred in every school play, and she posted videos of her short films online. She wanted to get into a good drama program in New York or LA or at Yale. But that was a whole year away. Right now, all she could do was perfect her acting and save money for school.

Bonnie was going to make it all the way. I just knew it. It was weird how I could be 100 percent sure of that and not at all sure for myself.

"Who cares about summer? This is it, Thea!"

"But . . ."

"No buts," she said with authority.

"This is your chance! Thea Roberts, fashion star! It's really happening."

"But what about you?" I blurted, pushing my baked french fries around with my finger.

"Me? I can take care of myself. Besides, now I won't have to compete with those twenty-foot legs of yours. Dom is all mine."

I looked up just as Bonnie broke into a smile. And I laughed, finally feeling it. Nothing really happened until I told Bonnie about it.

I was going to Los Angeles, to work for Lorelei Roy!

FOUR

When I got home, I found Gram in her studio. The attic smelled like oil paint, even with the windows open and a little fan blowing. On Gram's easel was the rough outline of a person's face in flesh-colored paint.

Gram looked up and smiled the smile that she reserved just for me. She adjusted her hair with her paint-covered fingers, then wiped her hands on her denim button-down.

I ran over and hugged her.

"What's gotten into you, Little Bean?"

I hadn't been little for a very long time. But I

was born premature, and the name stuck.

"You're getting paint all over yourself, Thea," Gram continued.

I squeezed her tighter. I didn't care.

* * *

The security guard nodded at me.

"You've only got ten minutes till closing," he warned with a smile.

DC is a city known for its politics, not its fashion, so most people probably don't go to the Smithsonian for its costume wing. I guessed that maybe I was its most frequent visitor.

I walked past the gowns of the First Ladies before reaching my final destination.

The dress was encased in glass. I had seen it the first time during a school tour of the Smithsonian. The other kids were interested in the presidential stuff. But I was all about the costume wing.

Michelle Obama's first inaugural dress was made out of cream silk. It was one-shouldered and elegant. And it had these gorgeous beaded flowers all over its flowing skirt. This dress represented a huge historical moment. One that I would never forget. The First Lady had used a new designer, Jason Wu. And in one night, Wu's whole life had changed, just like the new First Lady's did.

I whispered out loud to the dress. It was silly, but I did it anyway. "You won't believe it, but I'm going to LA."

I was ready.

FIVE

A guy at baggage claim stood holding a sign with my name on it.

My gram's extra-large pink suitcase was making its way around the baggage carousel. But I ignored it.

I couldn't stop staring at the guy with the sign. Because he was literally the best-looking person I'd ever seen in real life. Better looking than Dom. And he was waiting for me.

"Ms. Roberts," he said with a smile.

"Are you . . . him?"

I'd never seen a picture of Harmon Holt.

This guy didn't look quite right, though. He was well dressed and older. But he didn't look like a boss—much less the boss.

"I am not him," he said in a smooth New York accent. "But I work for him. You may call me Mr. Bosley. Think of me as H's right hand."

"I'm Thea. But you know that already," I stammered and then giggled.

"Which one is yours?" he asked.

I pointed out my bag, wanting to apologize for how ugly and heavy it was. My face suddenly felt warm from embarrassment.

Bosley picked it up effortlessly and led the way out of the airport. When Ms. Hampton told me that someone from Holt's staff would meet me, I guess I was expecting a secretary or an intern. Not Harmon Holt's right hand.

"Ms. Roberts, Mr. Holt is very impressed with you."

"Why?" I blurted.

He raised a perfect eyebrow.

"Why me?" I continued.

"H has an amazing track record. He's never been wrong."

"Oh," I said.

Bosley held the door for me as we headed toward a fancy SUV. I would have said more, but I was still trying to wrap my head around the idea that Harmon Holt had this much confidence in me.

Inside, I admired the interior of the nicest car I'd ever been in. Then I saw the Hollywood sign whiz by my window. I pressed myself closer to the SUV's window. Palm trees lined the streets. White stucco mansions with terra-cotta roofs sat on stone driveways.

"You'll be staying with a host family. They're friends of Holt Enterprises. They're happy to lend out their guesthouse."

Guesthouse? I thought I'd be staying in a dorm at one of the state colleges.

"Like charity," I said, sounding bitterer than I expected. I guess I'd been prepared for something different. A place with other kids.

"Like a favor for Mr. Holt. When Mr. Holt helps you, he expects nothing from you except to pay it forward."

"So this family I'm staying with, he helped

them once upon a time too?" I asked, filling in the fuzzy picture I had of Holt. Did the billionaire really spend all his spare time playing fairy godmother?

Bosley looked at me a long beat. I nodded as if I understood.

Harmon Holt had his name on buildings and planes and credits in movies and liner notes on albums. I wanted my name on one thing—those little labels that are sewn into the back of clothes. But wanting something and actually having something, like Harmon Holt did, seemed pretty far apart.

My jaw dropped when we pulled into the driveway of a huge house at the end of the block.

SIX

"You start work tomorrow at 7 a.m. sharp. Your host will drop you off. If you work past 9 p.m., Lorelei's company will provide a car. And here's a bus schedule, just in case."

I nodded at everything Mr. Bosley said. He got out and opened the door for me.

"Thank you for everything," I said, really meaning it.

He handed me a card with his info on it.

"If you need anything, reach out. Mr. Holt wants this to be a positive experience for all the interns involved."

I clutched the card in my hand as Bosley deposited me on the doorstep.

The door swung open. The inside of the house smelled like heaven—a breeze tinged with sugary sweetness.

A small, pretty woman with an open, round face and a tiny Afro stood in the doorway. She was wearing an apron. Was she the maid?

"Rebecca, this is Thea," Bosley said.

I couldn't help myself. "What is that smell?"

"I hope you like cupcakes," she answered.

* * *

It turned out that my host was Becca Grayson of Babycake Pops. She had started her business in her home kitchen, and she still used her kitchen to try out new designs and recipes.

Becca explained to me how she had left her career to start her own business. Now she was opening stores in twenty states. Bon and I had had her cake pops once at the mall back home. My favorite was mint chocolate chip. I couldn't believe that I was standing next to a cake pop mogul.

"I used to be a corporate lawyer. But once I had Molly, I took some time off, and Babycake was born. It's a pretty sweet life. Excuse the pun," she laughed. I wondered when we would get to the room where all the cooking magic happened.

She gave me the grand tour. Even though the house was fabulous, it looked lived-in. There were toys everywhere. When we finally reached the kitchen, there was a little girl, probably about five, sitting in a circle of stuffed animals. She ran up and hugged me.

"She never does that. She doesn't usually take to anyone this easily." Becca smiled wider.

"I've done a lot of babysitting," I replied. "Maybe she can sense it. If you ever need me to pitch in . . ."

"I might take you up on that, but my guess is you are going to be pretty busy with Lorelei. I really want you to feel like you're at home here. Now, Molly, let go of Thea so I can give her the rest of the tour."

I didn't mind really. I think I needed the hug.

Becca led me to the pool house, my home for the next month.

"All this is for me?"

"Unless you want to stay in the main house," Becca said. "We thought this would give you more privacy."

All this is for me, I repeated inside my head. It was like my own little apartment. There was an overstuffed sofa and a flat screen TV, a breakfast nook, and a full kitchen. A set of stairs inside the pool house led to a king-size bed and a dresser. And a bouquet of cake pops stood on a table next to the bed!

"The fridge is fully stocked. But we have dinner at eight, and we'd love for you to join us."

I nodded, still digesting the idea that I wasn't going to spend my summer in a dorm room. Instead, I'd have my own little corner of an estate.

"I'll give you some time to get settled."

Becca patted me on the shoulder and walked out with Molly trailing behind her.

I pulled my cell phone out of my bag and sank back onto the downy soft bed.

"You will not believe where I am."

SEVEN

"I can get here on my own next time," I said the next morning. Becca pulled up in front of the tall, lipstick-shaped building. The House of Lorelei Roy was on the fiftieth floor.

Becca shook her head. "It would take you three buses. And this place is on my way to the shop." She reached back to the backseat, where Molly was playing with a kid-sized laptop in her car seat. "Here."

She handed me a box of cake pops.

"Lunch?" I asked.

"No, for Lorelei—as a thank-you."

I entered the all-glass skyscraper, box in hand. My nerves began to kick in. What if they didn't like me? I looked down at my favorite dress for a boost of confidence. The paisley-printed, pink, pleated minidress had taken me hours and hours to get right. But it had been worth it. Every time I put on the dress, I felt pretty and powerful, like I could face anything.

A security guard directed me to the top floor. After a fifty-floor elevator ride, I stepped into the House of Lorelei Roy reception area. A pretty receptionist took my name and called someone named Jamie to get me.

Jamie had red hair cut into a severe bob, with those straight bangs that never look good on anyone with less-than-perfect bone structure. Jamie was that one in a million.

Although Jamie wasn't tall, she wore six-inch heels.

She looked at my feet immediately. "What size are you?"

"Size eight?"

"I'll lend you something from the closet."

It turned out that the comfortable two-inch heels I'd worn specifically for running around Lorelei's offices were completely out of place. I looked around. Everyone was wearing at least four inches.

Jamie led me to a main room filled with glass cubicles and girls dressed in Lorelei Roy's more affordable line.

"I'm Thea, the intern," I said.

"I know. Don't take offense about the shoes. We have one every season."

Did she really just say that? I had heard that fashion people could be brutal. I just didn't expect her to be so in-my-face about it.

"What are those?" Jamie asked.

"Cake pops. I'm staying with Rebecca Lawson. From Babycake Pops?"

Jamie shook her head as if to say I was completely in the wrong place and then took the pops from me.

"I brought those for Lorelei," I added.

"And if you give them to her, I'll be looking for another intern."

"They're gluten-free."

"Right now, Lorelei is food free. She's on a cleanse."

All I could manage was, "Oh."

***

Jamie absently tucked the cake pops under her arm and began a tour.

The LR logo was everywhere—monogrammed on the wallpaper, etched in glass on all the cubicles, even visible on the floor tiles. Jamie spotted me looking at the white-on-white embossed *L*s.

"The walls are also scratch and sniff," she said, and for a half second I thought she was being sarcastic. But I leaned in and scratched the wall anyway. It smelled like Lorelei's signature scent, Lavish—lilacs and lavender and some other sweet flower I didn't recognize.

Jamie's tour felt more like a lecture. She was showing me not just where things happened but what not to do when I got there. I wished I had brought a notebook to write all the don'ts down.

"Do not take pictures of anything we do here. Do not post anything to Twitter about our line unless we ask you to. We control the brand as much as we can. We make the message."

I nodded.

Jamie led me to the second most important room in the office: the coffee room.

"Lorelei has a double cappuccino with double foam. Skim milk. I'll show you how after you meet Lorelei."

Ms. Hampton had warned me that most internships involved a lot of menial labor. A small price to pay in exchange for total exposure to the inner workings of Lorelei's empire.

"PR, reception . . . ," Jamie announced, moving on.

She led me to another room with drafting tables and chairs. An iPad was docked at each station. Two guys sat in the room, probably both in their thirties. They could have been twins.

"There are three in-house designers in addition to Lorelei. That's Brandon and Jason. And yes, they are brothers. Lorelei likes having a matching set of designers. And here's Marnie. She's been with Lorelei from the beginning."

None of the designers looked up. They were

so absorbed in their work that they didn't even notice the interruption.

Next, Jamie led me to what she called the War Room. I was expecting a conference area. But it was a room full of fabric. There were three sewing room stations set up. No one was sitting at them.

"None of the designs are completed yet. So Paloma and Sophia have nothing to do yet. You'll meet them later."

When we got back to her desk, she handed me an iPad and an iPhone. I still sketched all my designs on paper, but Lorelei was apparently completely digital. I only had a second to contemplate sketching on a tablet before Jamie got down to business.

"Don't get too attached," she said. "You have to return them at the end of the summer."

EIGHT

Lorelei's office was literally the size of my house back in DC.

Lorelei run-walked into the room on a perfumed breeze. Lavish, of course. She circled around me like she was inspecting me. Her eyes traveled over my outfit.

"Nice lines. Excellent workmanship."

Lorelei Roy liked my dress! I felt the blood rush to my face.

I blurted out, "I made it," despite Jamie's order that I not speak unless Lorelei asked me to.

"Poor choice of fabric."

It still was a compliment. Sort of. Let the design speak for itself—that's what she meant.

She nodded at the door as if dismissing me.

I wanted to say something more. That I'd been looking at her designs in magazines for years. That I snuck into the library to watch her fashion shows on the computer during lunch during fashion week. That I was her biggest fan. But Jamie had given me instructions not to talk unless I was answering a question.

I turned and walked toward the door, but I couldn't stand it. Who didn't want to hear a compliment? She may be Lorelei Roy, but she was still a person.

I turned back.

"Ms. Roy, I just wanted to say . . ."

She looked up surprised, "Yes, Theresa?"

"It's, uh, Thea actually. I just wanted to say that it's a dream come true to work for you."

She studied me for a beat and then said, "Thea, sucking up isn't a requirement of this internship. Can you send Jamie in please?"

I nodded and walked out. The heels weren't the only part of me that hurt as I left the room.

* * *

I walked out of Lorelei's office feeling gut punched.

"Lorelei wants to see you," I told Jamie.

Either Jamie read my face or she knew that people typically needed to recover after meeting Lorelei. "Take ten minutes. Get to know the coffeemaker," she said.

Whatever sting I'd taken from Lorelei, I didn't have time to dwell on it. Madison Belle was sitting outside Lorelei's studio. The Madison Belle. Modeling superstar Madison Belle.

She was impossible pretty. My height but way more slender and graceful, like a ballerina or something. I was staring at her, but she was staring at a really cute boy who had leaned over one of the cubicles to grab a stapler. Another intern? A male model?

I must have been drooling.

"Look but don't touch," Madison warned as she turned her big green eyes on me. Boyfriend? Or had she just called dibs on a person?

Madison responded to my raised eyebrows. "He's just off-limits."

Before she could say more, Jamie reappeared and motioned to Madison. "Lorelei's ready for you," Jamie ordered with one hand on her barely-there hip. Then Jamie gave me a look that asked why I hadn't taken the break she'd ordered.

Following Jamie's orders, I headed for the coffee room. It was empty. After a couple of tries, I made a cappuccino with extra foam and sank into one of the white plastic chairs. I took a sip. If I was going to have to make the drink for Lorelei, I had to make sure that it tasted okay.

Mystery Boy entered, carrying a backpack and muttering to himself. He took a seat across from me, seemingly unaware that I was there.

I got up to leave, but he turned and started talking to me.

"You must hate her too."

"Hate who?"

"Lorelei Roy." He said as if everyone felt that way.

Was this a test?

I wasn't Lorelei's biggest fan at this exact moment. But I wasn't about to say that to a total stranger—no matter how dreamy he was.

"I have to go," I said. "My ten minutes are up."

They weren't, but I wasn't good at talking to boys. And I couldn't exactly figure out what his deal was.

"I hate her sometimes," he said.

"I'm sorry . . . What did she? . . . It's none of my business."

"It's less fun if you don't react," he added.

"Excuse me?"

"Lorelei. She's expecting you to crumble or pout or roll your eyes. But if you don't do any of those things, she'll move on to the next victim."

It was the same advice Gram used to give me about bullies—only I hadn't thought I'd need it at work.

"Thanks," I said, "I should really get back to my desk."

He dropped his backpack on the chair and stood up. "I'll go with you."

"Okay?"

The guy was even cuter up close. He had to be a model. But why was he walking me to my desk, which was directly across from Jamie's?

When we got to it, he asked me my name.

"I'm Thea. And you are . . . ?"

"I'm Matt."

With that, he was off. I heard him push open the door to Lorelei's office.

A voice boomed: "There he is. My pride and joy."

Who he was and why he was off-limits hit me like a truck. He was Lorelei's son.

* * *

The rest of the day was a blur. Everyone had a job to do, and there was little time to talk, so I had to learn by watching. And when there were breaks, everyone else seemed to have super-close relationships, complete with inside jokes. It wasn't that they were excluding me exactly. But they had their own rhythm. Or maybe they just didn't want to bother getting to know someone who would only be around for the summer.

I spent the car ride to Becca's house listening to her and Molly relive the highlights of their play date. I was happy not to talk about how my day went. I'd thought that fashion people would be *my* people, but it turned out the House of Lorelei Roy was a lot more complicated than that.

* * *

"How was your first day?" Becca asked from the kitchen.

Awesome, terrifying, terrible, I thought.

"It was cool."

First day. The only chance to make a first impression. But the only impression I had made so far was on Jamie, and I wasn't sure if it was a positive one.

"You want to try my new recipe?" Becca asked.

I said sure. As she handed me the cake pop, she added, "You want to talk about it?"

I shook my head no. And I took a huge bite. It tasted like a caramel sundae.

"How did you do that?" I asked.

"Magic," she laughed.

I could use a little of that, I thought.

NINE

The next day, around 4:30, Matt was in the break room again. I was there to make Lorelei's third cup of the day. I didn't bother to be coy. "Do you just come here every day to hang out with the models?"

"No, I have summer school," he said. "My mom wants to make sure I do my homework. So I do it here."

"What subject?" Was he one of those kids who didn't bother to study because he had everything?

"Test prep." He held up a book. It was the

same SAT book that Bonnie and I had shared this year.

"Mom wants me to go to an Ivy. And if I want a shot at that, I have to score well."

"And what do you want?" I asked. He didn't sound too interested in the future that his mom had planned for him. I had taken the SAT prep class voluntarily. Good test scores were still important to scholarship committees.

"No one ever asks me that," he said, looking surprised.

"Maybe you should be asking yourself that."

His face fell. Then he looked up at me with a smile. "Maybe I will."

"I took that same prep course last year. The key is to make flash cards."

"You took the course before?" Was that surprise, or was he just glad to meet someone else who had suffered through the same thing?

"Yeah, after school last semester. My best and I took it together. We made flash cards and practiced between work shifts. That way it feels more like a game than homework."

"Do you think maybe you could show me

your cards?"

"I don't have them with me. They're back in DC," I replied.

"Oh. Do you think you could show me your technique then? You'd be saving my life."

"Well, if it's a matter of life and death . . . Sure."

"What time does my mom set you free tomorrow?" he asked.

"Six," I said, unable to take my eyes off his.

"Can you stick around afterward?"

"But your mom—"

I was making it sound like we were planning something much more than a flash-card session.

"Right," he said as if he just remembered that Lorelei existed. "Okay. What about the Starbucks on the corner?"

"Okay. Tomorrow."

I walked out of the office carrying Lorelei's too-cold coffee.

* * *

I was smiling for the rest of the afternoon. Smiling while delivering mail, smiling while getting coffee, and smiling while running the copier. Even smiling when the copier jammed.

Jamie was still at her desk at six, when I was on my way out. I think she noticed my bubble and decided to burst it with a pile of extra work. "One last thing. Drop this in the trash room on your way out."

She held out three bolts of gorgeous silk.

"You're throwing that out?"

"Lorelei says that it should be burned. But the trash will have to do."

"But they're beautiful . . . "

She shrugged and went back to work.

I took the bolts down to the trash room. And gasped. The inside of the room looked like a dream. There were gorgeous silks and brocades, crisp cottons. Fabrics of every color and texture imaginable.

I left the bolts and began to walk away.

But when I got to the door, I turned back. I dug through the bin and pulled out a gorgeous pink charmeuse. It was just Lorelei's trash. But her trash was my treasure. And after a day of copying and coffee making, I needed some treasure.

***

During the car ride home, I told Becca that I didn't need a ride after work the next day.

"Making friends already?"

"Something like that," I said.

She smiled. "See, you have nothing to worry about."

When we got home, I finally called Bonnie.

"You have a date!" she squealed in my ear.

"It isn't a date. I'm just helping him with his flash cards. It's more a study date than a *date* date."

Bonnie laughed. "He could hire a tutor. He could hire a whole stack of tutors. He's like superrich."

"Maybe he just wants to ... I don't know. But it's not a date."

Bonnie started singsonging, "Matt and Thea sitting in a tree—"

"I'm hanging up now," I said, but I was smiling as I did.

TEN

After another day of Jamie's almost insults and more time with the copier, I walked into the Starbucks down the block.

I wasn't sure if I was imagining it, but it looked like Matt lit up when he saw me.

"Did you bring supplies?" I asked.

He looked at me blankly.

"For flash cards. You wanted me to help you with SAT prep?"

His eyebrows went up in surprise. "Oh, right. But I think we need to eat something first."

Maybe it *was* a date? An hour later, we were sitting on a curb, eating In-N-Out Burgers and looking off at the Hollywood sign. I still hadn't seen any sign of flash cards.

"Doesn't your mom want you to do whatever you want?" I asked between bites. "I mean, she does something creative for a living. Why not you?"

"Mom wants me to have a 'foundation.' Go to the best schools and I can do anything. That way, I won't have to struggle like she did."

"Lorelei struggled?"

"Mom started her business out of our fourth-floor walk-up when I was a baby. She'd gone to design school, but she built her business all on her own."

Everything I ever read about Lorelei was about her fabulous present. No one mentioned her past—her struggle. I had thought she was one of those overnight successes.

"Wow."

"If you tell her I told you, she'll kill you."

I nodded. So Lorelei hadn't always been Lorelei. Somehow knowing this made her a little bit less scary. And it made what I wanted seem a little bit more possible.

Matt pulled open the door of his blue convertible for me. I paused for a split second. I'd never had a guy hold open a door for me. Not on purpose.

Maybe he was just more polite than the guys back home? I was making myself more nervous.

Stay calm, be cool, be normal, I thought. Be in the moment.

I glanced at Matt's perfect profile as he stared at the road, and then I looked away again. It was too much. He snuck a look at me too. I looked out my window, pretending not to notice.

When we got to Becca's, I got out of the car before Matt could get around to it. But he still walked me to the door.

"Next time, you have to actually show me the flash card thing."

"Next time?"

"I didn't mean to presume . . . I just thought . . ." His eyes widened in confusion. Probably no one ever said no to him. Except his mom.

"Kidding," I said, tapping his shoulder.

He recovered and smiled broadly.

"I'll meet you tomorrow. Same time, same place."

He gave me a hug. He smelled like some cologne that none of the kids at Clinton wore. Hints of the woods and the ocean. He pulled away, and I realized I had closed my eyes to take in the scent.

I slipped inside the pool house and shut the door behind me. But the smell of the ocean—the smell of him—was still with me.

After I'd spilled every detail about my maybe date to Bonnie, I started to think about what Matt had told me about Lorelei. Then I took the scraps of fabric out of my bag and began to work on a new dress.

ELEVEN

The weird thing about fashion is that clothes are designed and sold a couple of seasons ahead. A spring line comes down the runway in the fall so that buyers and really rich people can see the clothes and decide what they want to buy. But Lorelei was designing a special "capsule" collection for teens, called *L is for Lorelei*. She wanted to launch with a rare summer showing. If the line were a success, it would become a regular part of Lorelei's collection.

At the meeting to plan that launch, my job was to pass out lunches without spilling anything on anyone famous. "Then you can be wallpaper and listen in," Jamie had told me, as though she were giving me the greatest gift ever.

And maybe it was a gift. By the second hour, the meeting was getting intense.

"We can do better than this, people!" Lorelei said, tapping her manicured nails against the glass desk. "I hear that Gwen Stefani will have a sushi conveyor belt for her launch. How do we compete with that?"

I tried to keep a straight face while stealing glances at Lorelei's so very serious one.

Lorelei wanted to brainstorm about a bird theme. Each model would represent a different bird. She wanted to make a statement about girls and individuality in the face of bullying. The girls would wear wings. It was a little silly but also really fun. I never really thought about what my clothes *meant*—other than "cute" or "hot" or "fun." But I guessed that what Lorelei was trying to do was say that the shows could mean something. They could be art.

Lorelei paused on Steffy Brown, a famous

makeup artist, and then Jadin Snow, a rock star hairstylist. "Steffy. Jadin. Ideas. What does this event look like?"

Steffy held up a drawing of an eye-shadowed model wearing a peacock print. Lorelei shook her head. They went around the table again and again, but Lorelei's reaction stayed the same. Nothing was quite good enough. I was glad I could stay safely in the background.

I had no idea what went into planning a fashion show. Lorelei had her hands on every detail, from the music to the design of the gift bags to the models' nail polish.

After a while, Lorelei said, "Let's move on. Jamie. What else? Where are we on a DJ?"

Jamie went over that and a half dozen other details, holding her tablet in one hand and sneaking peeks at Lorelei for approval.

Lorelei was decisive about everything. But she was also surprisingly open to suggestions. She seemed to want them—even if she had no problem saying a suggestion sucked. I liked her better by the end of the meeting. Not that I was any less clammed up by the time it finished.

I wondered if you had to be that tough to get anywhere in the fashion business.

***

"It's like planning a fifteen-minute prom," I blurted to Jamie as we finally left the conference room. I was balancing a three-foot stack of binders. Jamie's hands were completely free. She didn't offer to help, not that I expected her to.

Although Jamie rarely spoke back, I'd decided to keep trying to have a conversation with her. When she did answer, it was usually because she thought I was wrong about something. Like the time after the meeting.

Jamie shook her head like I was hopeless. Her flawless hair didn't move. "It's more like planning a fifteen-minute TV commercial. You want it to feel like a party, but you also want them to go home and think about the clothes, and then go buy a little of that magic."

What she said made sense. We were making clothes to sell them. Not just as a project for us. But as I looked at Lorelei stiletto her way down the hall, I felt sure it was more than that to her.

***

Once the day was finished, I sat down at one of the sewing machines in the workroom. Nobody had used the machines the entire time I'd been at the House of Lorelei Roy, so I figured it wouldn't be a problem. Becca didn't have a machine at her house, and I was actually ready to start sewing the dress I'd been designing. I could already sense that it was going to be the best dress I'd ever made. Lorelei was right— having the right fabric made all the difference.

After twenty minutes of sewing, I leaned back in the chair and looked at my work. "Not bad," I said to myself.

Just then, the door swung open.

TWELVE

Jamie stood in the doorway, looking at the dress and then at me.

"I knew it." She said it like she had been expecting me to fail.

"I just saw all the fabric in the trash. I hated for it to go to waste."

I reached for the dress, but Jamie was faster than me. She scooped it up and took a step away from me.

"It's stealing. And I'm telling Lorelei." She sounded like a ten-year-old ready to tattle, but I knew the situation was more serious than that.

"You were throwing it away," I said. "It's not like I was hurting anyone."

My internship was over. My life was over.

"Tell it to security," Jamie said, pulling her phone out of her pocket and unlocking it.

My first mug shot flashed before my eyes. Bonnie would be so disappointed. Gram would be so disappointed.

I gulped, swallowing a "please." But "please" wouldn't work on Jamie. "Please" would just be fuel for the fire. There was nothing I could do. Nothing I could say. Jamie had wanted me gone, and I'd given her the perfect weapon to get rid of me. I looked at the dress, still in her metallic-nailed clutches. She was dialing her phone with the other hand.

And then things got really weird.

"Jamie!" boomed a voice from the hall. "Where are you?"

Lorelei.

Jamie smiled. Security had nothing on Lorelei.

"In the workroom," Jamie answered.

Lorelei strode in, and Jamie didn't waste a

moment. "Our intern was stealing, Lorelei."

She pointed at me, and my dress seemed to catch Lorelei's eye. Jamie hissed something about me being a Dumpster-diving thief, but I could see Lorelei was only paying attention to the half-finished dress.

"Shut up for a second, Jamie," Lorelei commanded. Lorelei looked into my eyes as though she was seeing me for the first time.

"You can rummage through my trash anytime you want," Lorelei said. "But I'd much rather see what you can do with this."

She turned around, picked up a piece of white lace, and handed it to me.

I took it, inhaling deeply.

"It's for the new line. I want you to fit Madison."

Lorelei turned on her heel and walked out. Jamie could only manage to say "But—!"

I waited until she huffed out behind Lorelei to let myself smile.

THIRTEEN

"This one is easy. *Tensile* means a) stressful, b) outdated, or c) stretchable."

The day after Jamie found me in the workroom, Matt and I were sitting at Becca's kitchen table, finally going over flash cards. Molly was at the other end of the table coloring in a coloring book. Matt looked at her like he'd rather be doing what she was doing.

"C." He said.

"Right. That's twenty out of twenty."

He put up his hand for a fist bump.

After we ate some cupcakes—too many—to

celebrate the perfect score, I walked Matt to the door, and he thanked me. I wondered if this was it. If he no longer had an excuse to hang out with me.

"I owe you one," he said.

"No, you don't. It was fun."

"I always pay my debts. I'll pick you up tomorrow. After work. "

Not good-bye after all.

FOURTEEN

When I stepped into the studio, Madison Belle was already there. She gave me a look that was somewhere between surprise and recognition. Did she remember warning me about Matt?

"I'm Thea. I'm supposed to help you with your fitting."

I still couldn't believe it. And neither could Jamie, who had been sulking all week. She had totally expected me to be carted off to juvie for using a few scraps of fabric. For a few minutes, I had expected the same thing.

"I'm Madison," she said, as if anyone who

ever opened a fashion magazine didn't already know her name. "Call me Mad. My friends do."

I had expected cell-phone-throwing diva behavior. Instead, she had just called me a friend. I laughed, a little nervously. Madison—Mad—seemed like a regular girl, but I couldn't completely forget that I was talking to a supermodel.

Jamie had given me instructions for working with Madison. They were remarkably similar to those that she'd given to me about Lorelei. Don't ask too many questions; be invisible. But Madison had started the conversation with me. It would be rude not to talk back.

"Um. Is it true you dated Justin Bieber?"

"Not true. But we have the same stylist. He gave me a lift on his private plane. Absolutely nothing happened except him talking about how awesome his current girlfriend was for like seven hours. It was nauseating."

Madison's stories were a lot different from mine. Losing a shoe on the runway in Milan. Going to sleep on a train in London on the way to a show and ending up in Liverpool. Supermodel problems.

I spotted Matt through the glass wall as Madison stepped down from the fitting podium. He waved at me, and I waved back.

Madison arched a perfectly tweezed eyebrow. "You didn't."

"I don't know what you're talking about," I lied.

"Just keep it on the DL. Or Lorelei will kill you."

I wanted to hate Madison. But she was so different than I had expected. She was funny and nice and real, despite the fact that I was sewing her into a dress that cost more than Gram's rent.

While I worked away, Madison told me all about her runway-walking roommates.

"Like *America's Top Model*," I said, "only no one gets kicked out every week."

"Not exactly, but we do compete: Who books the most print? Who books the most runway? Who walks the best?. Who has the best billboard placement?" She wasn't bragging. This was just her reality. Her supermodel reality.

There were downsides, though. "Once one of my roomies switched out all my clothes with smaller sizes," Madison said. "I dieted for a week."

"That doesn't sound funny. It sounds mean," I blurted out.

Madison's face dropped as if I had given the wrong response. But my gut said I was right. The model house was playing its own twisted Hunger Games. "Why don't you get your own place? They sound like monsters."

She shrugged. "They're my monsters. Five girls in the same apartment means regularly scheduled catfights. But I met these girls when I was fresh off the Greyhound. They know me and I know them. And in this town, that's worth a few scratches."

I nodded, thinking of Bonnie. "I have a friend like that back home."

"Good for you. You're lucky." There was something a little sad about the way she said it.

FIFTEEN

"It's reaping day," Jamie said, almost smiling up at me. She was in an unusually good mood as I pushed the mail cart past her desk. I was in a good mood too. Something about Matt's wave in front of Madison the day before.

Jamie probably expected me to be clueless, but Mad had told me what "reaping day" was. On reaping day, we picked the rest of the models for the *L is for Lorelei* launch. Madison was a lock as model-slash-muse. But the rest of the show hadn't been booked yet.

Fifteen minutes later, we were standing at a

long table in Lorelei's private studio.

Jamie told me to take notes if I wanted. But my main job was to mark which girls were "yeses" and which were "nos."

The models called the appointments "gosees." Girls walked in at fifteen-minute intervals. They tried on a couple of dresses and walked the length of the conference room while we sat and passed judgment. Jamie led the girls in and out.

They all walked in wearing the same uniform of jeans, some kind of T-shirt, and hair pulled up in a high pony or blown off the face. Blank canvases for Lorelei to paint on.

The second the door slid shut, Lorelei made proclamations. And the other people at the long table sucked up, agreeing with her. It was a series of Goldilocks moments—too big, too small, etc. No model was just right!

Which was weird, because each girl that came in was prettier than the last.

"I like her, but I don't know if she's got the build for the teen line . . ." Lorelei paused. "She's a no."

But she's a teenager, I thought. She's sixteen. How can she not be right for it? But I kept my lips sealed shut.

When there was only one girl left, I sighed and glanced down at all the nos on my tablet. When I looked up, Lorelei was staring at me.

"Write this down: tell the agent that we love her, but we need to be sure that she stays true to the brand."

Is that code for not gaining a pound? I wondered.

Lorelei stopped. "What is it, Thea?"

"I didn't say anything." I said, feeling the blood rush to my face. "I was just wondering . . . Is there a reason why we can't have more girls who look like girls?"

Lorelei began to laugh. Jamie looked like she was going to die.

"We want to showcase the designs in the best possible light. I'm creating a moment of perfection. *Any* Lorelei Roy show is a moment of perfection."

"But nobody's perfect," I said under my breath.

But Lorelei was looking into the doorway. "She is."

Lorelei wasn't wrong. The girl in the doorway looked like a young Naomi Campbell. Perfect skin and hair to her waist. She also had a body that owned the room like no one else had.

I looked down at the list again and put a check next to Brie Summers's name.

* * *

Later that day, Madison pumped me for info about the day's model massacre.

"They did pick one girl," I reported. "Brie something?"

Her eyes lit up like she knew the name.

"Not Brie Summers," Madison said.

"Yeah, do you know her?"

She nodded. "She's one of my roommates."

SIXTEEN

When Brie showed up the next morning, she and Madison greeted each other with air kisses.

Mad introduced me as "the coolest girl ever." I smiled automatically, surprised by Mad's compliment. Brie looked me over like she was making a decision.

"I got here just in time," Brie said to Madison. "You poor thing, you're actually making friends with the interns."

Mad cast an apologetic glance in my direction, then said to Brie, "You just bring happiness and light with you wherever you go."

Brie shrugged. "Can your new bestie get me a bottle of water?"

"Get it yourself," Mad insisted.

"I don't mind." I got up, not wanting to wait on some diva but wanting out of the room for at least a second. I ran right into Matt.

"Tough day?" he asked.

"I have to go get Princess Brie some water."

"I'll go with you. I'm thirsty too."

When I got back with a water bottle, Brie was gone. Brie didn't like me and for no particular reason. At least nothing that I could pinpoint.

"Ignore her. It's not you. She hates everyone."

"Why?"

"Because she wants to be the next Naomi Campbell or something. Giselle's the body, Kate's the Face, Naomi Campbell's the Walk, and Brie's going to be the Wicked Witch of the Runway."

"And what are you?" I asked.

"I don't know—I guess I was hoping that I'd just be me."

"The Madison?"

She laughed.

* * *

"Maybe she doesn't like you because you get to eat and she doesn't," Bonnie suggested on the phone later.

"Not funny," I laughed. But it caught somewhere in the back of my throat. It sounded a little too true.

SEVENTEEN

The next couple of weeks went by quickly. Lorelei held fittings and chose the rest of the girls. Meanwhile, I spent almost every other night either working on my trash-bin dress or hanging out with Matt, and every day either completing menial tasks for Jamie or making alterations on the dress Mad would wear in the show.

The competition didn't bring out the best in the models. Madison was less talkative than at the start of the summer, and I thought she was getting even thinner.

* * *

When I got back from the break room from accidentally on purpose having lunch with Matt, the main office was empty.

I could hear Jamie's voice coming from inside Lorelei's studio. She was threatening someone: "If you don't come out, I'm calling security,"

Brie's voice slinked through the bathroom door. "Go ahead."

Brie had locked herself in, and she wasn't coming out.

"Couldn't zip the dress," Marnie whispered.

"Can we let it out?" I asked, wondering what the big deal was. We still had ten days till the show.

"We already did."

I'd noticed that Brie had gained a little weight. Everyone had noticed. But I didn't think it was a big deal. Maybe Brie just wanted a little attention, like Mad said.

"Maybe we should just give her some space," Brandon proposed.

"We need the dress," Jamie said. "Lorelei will be back from lunch soon. We have fifteen minutes tops." She picked up the phone—she was considering calling security.

I wondered if Jamie called security when the printer ran out of ink.

But she was right. If Lorelei came back and found Brie locked in the bathroom, she'd freak. "Let me try," I offered, surprising myself. I walked up to the door and whispered loudly, "Are you okay?"

"Is that you, intern girl?" Brie asked.

She opened the door a crack and pulled me inside. She locked it behind me.

Brie's mascara was running down her face and threatening to smudge the dress she was wearing. My job was to get it off of her without leaving a mark. And she knew it.

"Take your stupid dress," Brie said. "I know that's all you care about."

Brie slipped out of the dress and pulled on her red high heels. Then she grabbed her trench coat, threw it over herself, and stormed through the showroom. She didn't even bother going back to her dressing room for her clothes.

A piece of paper fluttered to the floor. I picked it up.

It read, "Don't feed the models."

EIGHTEEN

Bon laughed as she answered her phone. "What's up, Fashion Star? Dom says hi."

"Seriously?" I asked, forgetting for a sec about the locked studio incident.

"We're going out to see a movie," Bon said. "I told him how lonely I was without my BFF, and he said we should do something. So he's picking me up after work to see that new movie musical."

"OMG. That's awesome."

"You're sure you're okay with it?"

"Yeah, I'm sure," I said, smiling.

My crush on Dom had faded the second I met Matt. I was happy for Bon.

"You don't sound sure. You sound sad."

"Oh no, it's not you or you and Dom. It was the reaping and everything after."

"Excuse me?"

I filled her in on Brie's sudden, half-naked exit from the House of Lorelei Roy.

"It was brutal, Bon. These girls—I felt so badly for them," I said.

"But no one's forcing them to do it, right? It's hard to feel bad for supermodels."

But for me, it wasn't that hard anymore. The more I thought about Brie, the worse I felt.

* * *

I couldn't even concentrate on my work. My brain kept circling back to the image I had of Brie running out of the dressing room in her trench coat. The next time I saw Madison, it was hard to keep quiet.

"It wasn't fair," I said.

"What?"

"What happened to Brie."

"You don't even like Brie."

"I know, but . . ."

"It's the business," Mad said. "If you choose to be a model, being thin is part of the job."

Before I could say something more, Madison had spotted the trash-bin dress sticking out of my bag.

She pulled it out and spun it around. "Love it. Can I have it?"

I told her the whole story about the dress and my "punishment."

"Well, the trash room's loss is the fashion world's gain," Mad said.

I shrugged. "I have a million miles to go before I'm Lorelei."

"Don't be so sure. One piece of clothing could change your whole life."

I looked at Mad skeptically.

"I owe my whole career to a pair of snake-print leggings," she said. "One time, me and my friend Mercy were walking through the mall, like we did every weekend. There was absolutely nothing else to do on a Saturday in Camden, Wisconsin. And we were about to leave, but suddenly I decided I *had* to go back and try on these leggings I'd seen in the window of the Gap. Mercy didn't want to walk all the way back, but I insisted.

"So I was going through this pile of leggings, looking for my size, and this woman walked right up to me and asked if I'd ever thought about modeling. I thought she was kidding at first. But she had this business card that looked really official, so I did what she said. I took it home and gave it to my mom. And three months later, I walked my first runway in New York. That's where Lorelei spotted me. She asked me to be the face of the new teen line. I've always loved her clothes, so here I am.

"The truth is, I had never thought about modeling, but I *had* thought about getting out of Wisconsin. And I'd thought of traveling—but this life wasn't my dream. I owe it all to a pair of leggings I didn't even buy."

It was weird. Both Matt and Mad were living lives that had never been part of their dreams, while I'd been kind of obsessed with my dream since I was six.

"I can't imagine having someone walk up to me like that," I said.

Madison shrugged. "Isn't that kind of like what happened to you with Harmon Holt? He scouted you, just like that model scout scouted me."

Was she right? In a weird way, Madison and I weren't that different. Only Mad had already made it, and I was just starting. And there was absolutely no guarantee I would ever be the success story that she was.

"You're in the room. You're working at Lorelei Roy. Sure, luck and timing mean something. But all you can do is strut your stuff and see what happens. And by strut your stuff, I mean finish that dress."

NINETEEN

Brie didn't come back for her next fitting. A girl named Maggie replaced her. Maggie was half the girl Brie was—literally.

And I wasn't sure it was real or if I was imagining it, but things felt different after Brie left. Everyone was on edge. Especially Madison.

"Are you okay?" I'd ask her.

"I'm fine."

But Mad wasn't. I just didn't know how not fine she was.

One day, when I got back from restocking the copy room, I found Madison crumpled on the floor of a fitting area in her underwear, her dress lying beside her. She wasn't moving.

I ran over and knelt beside her. She was breathing. I shook her. Her eyes opened.

"I'm going to go get some help," I said.

"Don't," she whispered, sitting up. She was blinking rapidly as if trying to focus.

"But . . . you need a doctor or something."

"Forgot to eat," she said. "I'm fine. Really."

She got back up on her feet, but she still seemed a little unsteady. I grabbed a bottle of water and handed it to her.

"See, I'm fine." She took a sip and twirled around wobbly.

"You just fainted. You're not fine."

"Please don't tell anyone," Mad said, her eyes pleading with me. "This is my life. My career. Everything."

* * *

After Mad left the House of Lorelei Roy, I paced the fitting room. I wanted to call Bon. But she was probably out with Dom. I tried Gram next.

Gram wasn't like other grandmothers. She

didn't bake cookies or cook. But she was always there for me. She picked up on the first ring.

"How's the City of Angels treating my girl?"

"It's great, Gram."

"Really? That's why you're calling outside our designated calling time?"

Even if Gram couldn't see me, she still knew me so very well.

"It's nothing. I'm fine Gram. I just wanted to hear your voice."

"Now I know there's something wrong. You used the F-word."

Fine was a four-letter word in our house. Gram thought it was lazy. She wanted me to use my words like colors on canvas or pieces of fabric. She expected me to paint a picture.

I launched into a description of Becca's place to distract her: "The house is awesome, and you should see the studio . . ."

But Gram wasn't buying it. "The politics of the workplace aren't always easy. You have to know when to put your head down and when to speak up."

Grandma sold her paintings to a little gallery downtown, but her art wasn't enough to support us. She had also worked as a secretary for like a million years at a big insurance company before retiring a year ago.

I couldn't imagine her keeping her head down. Gram said exactly what she was thinking all the time.

"It's going okay," I said. "It's just different than I thought."

"I know it will be okay. Dreaming is the easy part, Little Bean. There's a reason it's called work."

"I know, Gram. And I'm actually okay with that part. I don't mind it, at least."

She pressed me: "Then what?"

"I made a friend. And now I think I'm losing her."

Gram didn't preach. She listened. A few seconds before she hung up, she said only, "Being a friend isn't just about being liked."

When I hung up, I felt warm and comforted. It had nothing to with the California sun bearing down on me. I didn't know what I was going to do, but for a moment at least, I felt better.

TWENTY

I wasn't a snitch. But keeping Madison's secret felt like watching a time bomb that was bound to go off.

"What's wrong, Little Bean?" Matt said with a throaty laugh as we sat on our spot in view of the Hollywood sign.

I threw my sandwich at him, and he caught it effortlessly.

Matt had been calling me that since he overheard Gram on the phone the last time he and I were together. I pretended to hate it, but I didn't.

"What if you knew something about someone, but you could cost them their job if you told someone else?"

"If it's Jamie, then tell Lorelei." He pulled out his phone. "I'll call her now if you want."

I'd told Matt about the time Jamie threatened to call security on me. If he hadn't liked Jamie before, he liked her even less now. He was definitely Team Thea. I didn't know what else we were, though. Friends? More than friends?

I shook my head. "It's not Jamie."

"Is this hypothetical person in any danger?"

"Maybe."

"Then I think you have your answer."

He didn't sound preachy. He sounded right. Madison was going to hate me. But at least she'd be alive to do so.

* * *

"So I went through my closet, and I found a few things that are perfect for you. Can you use these? Work your magic." Madison towered over me, holding two shopping bags filled to the brim with clothing.

I opened one of the bags. They didn't need my magic. The tags were still on some of the items. Was she trying to buy my silence?

"I can't take these."

"Of course you can," Mad said. "No one says no to Gucci. That's like a fashion crime or something."

"Are you doing this so I won't say anything?"

"Say anything about what?" She blinked innocently. Then her face darkened. "I'm doing this because I thought we're friends."

"And that's why I'm—look, Mad. I really think you should talk to somebody. If you don't, I will."

"You'll do what, exactly? Tell Lorelei? Do you think she'll even care? Thea, you *can't*. Did you see what happened to Brie? That's not going to happen to me."

"Something worse could happen to you. I looked online—what you're doing to your body—it could damage your heart. You could die."

"Don't be so dramatic."

"At least see somebody," I said. "A doctor or a nutritionist or a psychiatrist."

"Psychiatrist? So you're saying I'm *crazy*? Some friend," she said and stormed out.

The thing about giving an ultimatum was that I had to be prepared if Mad called my bluff.

I headed for Lorelei's office. Jamie stopped me, without looking up from her desk. "Where do you think you're going?"

"I need a minute with Lorelei."

"No one gets a minute with Lorelei unless Lorelei requests it."

"But there's something she needs to know. It's about Mad."

Jamie rolled her eyes. "It's Madison's job to be thin. Do you really think that Lorelei doesn't know? Let it go, intern. Find something to copy."

I walked away feeling worse than ever. I had tried. But had I tried hard enough?

TWENTY-ONE

The next morning, Lorelei found me in the sewing room. I had her permission to work on my design before and after work.

"I'd use a box stitch," she said from the doorway.

I opened my mouth to tell her about Madison. But her stern expression made me keep my mouth shut.

"You understand that I like to keep my work life separate from my personal life."

Had someone told her I'd been spending time with Matt?

"Either you're part of the personal or you're part of the professional—it's your choice." Lorelei used the same voice she used when she wanted me to do something small, like get her cappuccino with extra foam. But this was definitely a threat.

"Don't bother coming in tomorrow," she said as she examined the hem of my dress.

The white floor seemed to drop out beneath me. Was my internship really over because I spent a little time with her son? I wasn't even sure what Matt and I were yet.

"I want you to spend the day at the store instead. Tell Jamie to make arrangements."

* * *

It wasn't too harsh a punishment. I liked the store and its manager. She was pretty and polished and bore a remarkable resemblance to Lorelei. I organized shelves, inventoried clothes, and rung up a couple of customers. But I missed having a coffee break with Matt. I missed working on my dress. I even missed Mad, although I was pretty sure she had told Lorelei about me and Matt.

When I walked outside to walk to the bus stop, I was surprised to see Matt's car outside.

"Hop in," he commanded.

'What are you doing here?" I asked.

"Paying you back."

"How did you know where I was?"

"Madison told me."

I smiled and pushed aside the nagging feeling that this might be the last time I hung out with Matt.

Might as well enjoy it, I thought.

* * *

"I never do the touristy stuff. You give me a good excuse to be a little lame," Matt said as I put my hands into the handprints of Kristen Stewart.

We were at the TCL Chinese Theatre. There were foot and handprints from tons of famous people on the ground, from an old movie star like Joan Crawford to Will Smith. Matt knew a lot about the movies. Even the really old ones.

"Are you calling me lame?" I asked.

"You're not from here. It's cool for you to do all the Disney stuff. But as a native, it's so not cool."

"So you're just using me so you can be a tourist again."

Matt laughed and offered his arm. Which could have been a lame move, but when he did it, my heart sped up.

"You seem to know a lot about this movie stuff," I said. "Have you ever thought . . . ?"

His eyes lit up a little. "Yeah, maybe . . . I have written a few things in class . . . drama stuff . . ."

He looked off toward the horizon.

"You've written a few things, like what?" I said.

"Just some stuff. I'll show you sometime—"

"I'd love that."

"—If and only if you do something for me."

I was suddenly aware of how close we were. Of Matt's hand on my arm.

"Anything."

"Tell me what happened today," he said.

I released his arm.

I sighed. I had put the future on the table. He had every right to ask about the present.

"I think she knows. Your mom."

"Knows what?"

"About us."

He raised an eyebrow. Maybe I shouldn't have said "us."

"I mean, I think she knows about you and me spending time together."

"She doesn't know. I'd know if she knows. Mom's not exactly subtle."

"She practically spelled it out before she sent me to the retail store for the day."

Matt's face broke with what looked like relief.

"Is that all? Mom makes everyone work in the store for a day. She made me work in the store once. Best and worst day of my life. All those girls—but all those clothes . . ."

He laughed. I didn't.

"Thea, Mom doesn't keep secrets. If she'd mad at you, she's right in your face."

I shook my head.

"Then what do you want to do about it?"

Matt said. "Never see each other again?"

I shook my head again. "Is that what you want?"

"No."

"So what do we do?" I asked.

"We just have to be a little more discreet. Mom is so busy with the line, there's no way she'll ever know for sure."

I knew that Lorelei would make time to find out about us. But I didn't want to give Matt up either.

TWENTY-TWO

My next fitting with Madison was completely silent. I still couldn't believe she had told Lorelei my secret. But what other explanation was there?

When I was finished, Madison stormed out without saying a word. Jamie entered the fitting area and studied me a beat. "Is Madison mad?"

"Someone told Lorelei about me spending time with Matt."

"And you think it was Mad."

I shrugged.

"No one cares about your puppy love, sweetie. And anyway, no one would've had to tell her.

These walls are made of glass. Lorelei sees everything around here."

Jamie put me on phone duty while she handled something in Lorelei's office. When her phone rang, I reached over the desk to grab it—and a portfolio spilled onto the floor. I picked it up.

The drawings were modern and sleek, even a little goth. They had little in common with the tightly wound fashionista in front of me.

"Don't touch those," Jamie's voice broke in.

"You did these? These designs are amazing."

A look of what must have been pride crossed Jamie's face before she shifted to her usual pout.

"What do you think I'm doing here? You think that I get off on getting yelled at?"

"Have you shown them to Lorelei?"

"The only thing Lorelei is interested in is the pretty graph I've made of her schedule."

I looked at Jamie again, as if for the first time. I'd never asked Jamie what she was doing working for Lorelei. She hadn't exactly given me an opening. But I tried to put myself in her six-inch Louboutins. Jamie had been slaving away as Lorelei's first assistant for how long?

And even though I was just an intern, Lorelei had already given me feedback on my designs.

"You have no idea how this business works," Jamie said. "There's a whole lot of ugly beneath the prettiness. And you have to be willing to do whatever it takes. If it means starving yourself or being a royal witch or waiting behind a desk for years, then you do it. And you don't ask questions or whine about what's fair."

One design remained on her desk, a sketch of a purply-pink jumpsuit that shouldn't have worked but was somehow beyond cool. Jamie grabbed it and began to move off.

Everything Jamie had said sounded way too true. Everyone kept saying, "It's the business," as an excuse for all the crappy stuff that went down in fashion. But no one did anything to change it. Maybe there was no way anyone could. Maybe fashion changed you.

For the first time since I first picked up a needle, I wondered if I really, really wanted to do this.

TWENTY-THREE

The day of the show, I walked into the main house still wearing my pajamas and took in the smell of Becca's pancakes. I took a seat in front of a huge chocolate chip stack. Becca was hanging over the grill, humming a Rihanna song as she flipped another pancake.

"You ready for today?"

I nodded.

I wasn't really ready. And I wondered if I'd been wrong about everything. Maybe I should have talked to Lorelei about Madison's problem—maybe not talking *was* the problem. After the show, I would. I wasn't giving up. And I wasn't walking away, not yet. I'd been working on the launch all summer. I had to see it through.

* * *

My job was supposed to be to put a gift bag in every seat. I turned over the card in my hand to see it was marked with the name of *Vogue*'s editor in chief. A hot celebrity couple would be seated in the front row.

My stomach did flips.

As the show started, Lorelei's works came to life. But Madison was missing from the lineup. She had been assigned three looks. And Maggie was wearing the first one.

I got a text from Jamie from backstage.

"She wants you," Jamie squawked in my earpiece. "Says she's not feeling well. She's just going to do the showstopper. She probably needs help with the dress. Diva moment. Go."

"She asked for me?"

"*Yes*," Jamie said. "Make up, and get her on the runway."

All the other models dressed in an open area

backstage with the help of the other assistants, but Madison had her own space. I took a deep breath before I entered. Madison was dressed in street clothes.

"What's going on?" I said.

She had a little Band-Aid on her forehead. Brie was standing beside her, leaning against the floor-to-ceiling mirror.

"I fainted again," Madison murmured. "Brie took me to the ER last night."

"Oh, Madison." I felt gut punched. Was this my fault?

Madison shook her head. "I'm fine. Okay, I'm not fine. But I will be. We can throw me a pity party later. Anyway, I'm not doing the show. You are."

"What are you talking about? There's no way I can fit in that dress."

"But you can fit this one."

Madison pulled another dress out of her bag: the one I'd been working on. I'd left it in the dressing room when she and I had our big fight. Madison must have scooped it up. "You were saying how there should be real dresses for real girls. You're the real girl."

"I couldn't."

"I have a car waiting to take me to Renew. Brie's coming with."

"The rehab center?"

My first thought was the wrong one: couldn't Mad wait fifteen minutes before she got help?

"Couldn't Brie . . . ? I could go with you."

Brie shook her head, "I couldn't. I'm doing Marc's show tomorrow. Exclusive contract."

"So did you mean all that stuff you said, or didn't you?" Madison said. Her tone was harsh, but there was need underneath it. She was taking a big leap, getting help. She needed to know I was serious about trying to make things better for models.

"Okay. I'll do it."

Brie helped me into the dress. "There. Perfect. Now let's get some makeup on you."

"This is crazy."

Before Mad slipped out of the dressing room she said, "Good luck."

"You too," I said.

And then she was gone.

TWENTY-FOUR

I could hear Jamie shrieking backstage: "Madison, you're up!"

This was not the way I imagined my first runway show. Lorelei was going to kill me. I was probably going to never work in Los Angeles—or any town—again. But it was worth it.

"You're not Madison," Jamie said, moving her headset down so she could yell at me.

"Mad's getting help. She wanted me to take her place."

I wondered if I could run past Jamie. Would she physically try and stop me? She was super tiny, but maybe she had crazy-rage strength.

But Jamie stepped aside.

"If Lorelei asks, I had nothing to do with this," she said. "Now, remember, be fierce. Toe-heel, toe-heel . . ."

* * *

There was an audible gasp as I made my way down the runway. The path seemed to get longer with every step. I toe-heeled like I'd seen Madison and the other girls do in the showroom. But it felt different with a hundred eyes watching me.

When I finally reached the end of the runway, where a nest of photographers sat waiting, I pivoted one of my hips forward and paused. I gave my best smile as the flashbulbs went off.

Beyond the cameras, I caught a glimpse of Lorelei, her eyes narrowed on me. Her mouth was fixed in a smile that wasn't real.

"Thea!"

Someone was calling my name. Matt.

Matt was pushing through the photogs and trying to reach me.

"What are you doing?" I asked.

By the time he was standing next to me, I could see Lorelei's face flinch.

"You asked me if I knew what I wanted," Matt said simply. "You are what I want."

He slipped his hand into mine. The rest of the world slowed down while my pulse quickened. And with that, he kissed me.

I could still hear the cameras going off, but my eyes were closed. Matt was kissing me. My heart was bounding against my chest.

In my head, I was already composing the text I was going to send to Bonnie. This was really happening.

TWENTY-FIVE

When the show was over, Matt was still holding my hand. Lorelei spoke with a few members of the press, then made her way to us.

She said through clenched teeth, "Matthew. Home. Now."

He didn't move.

She looked at me. "My office. Fifteen minutes."

I looked at Matt. "It's fine. I'm okay. Go. "

* * *

Fifteen minutes later, I stood in Lorelei's

all-white office, waiting for her to make my termination official.

"Do you know how many people depend on me? Do you know what happens to them if this line isn't a success?"

Lorelei's whole company rode on every show. Had I put all that in jeopardy? If the House of Lorelei Roy took a hit, wouldn't it be her employees that really got hurt? If the presence of one average girl on the runway could jeopardize an entire business, there was something totally screwed up about that. Could my extra ten pounds really topple an entire empire?

"What do you think would have happened to the new line if Madison fainted on the runway?" I said, teetering a little in my heels as I spoke.

Lorelei didn't blink. "There will always be a place for Madison at Lorelei Roy. I only wish that she or you had come to me with your concerns about her health."

Would she have really helped Madison? Did she really not know? I wasn't sure. Maybe I should have come to Lorelei. Maybe Madison should have.

"If you want to make this up to me and to everyone at the company, then you'll need the remainder of the summer to do it."

"Excuse me?" I said. "You're not firing me?"

"I'd like you to continue helping with the teen line. You're undisciplined, but you have talent. Personally, I think that your little stunt was reprehensible—"

I wasn't going to apologize. But I hadn't thought about her new line being at stake. I hadn't thought about all the people that I'd spent the last month working with.

"But the bloggers at *Teen Dream* loved it," Lorelei continued. "One of them tweeted that it was a stroke of genius. And she's not completely wrong. There's something there. And like I said, you owe this company now. If you finish out August with no other incidents like this one, there may be a paid position for you here next summer."

"I don't know what to say."

"A smart girl would say yes, but take your time."

I walked out of the room feeling more confused than ever.

TWENTY-SIX

Mad's treatment center wasn't just for kids who were too skinny. It was also for kids with other troubles. I don't know what I'd expected. Kids walking around in those hospital robes that flashed everyone in the back. But the place wasn't like that at all.

In the rec room where Madison was allowed to have visitors, everyone was fully dressed and hanging out. I wouldn't have been able to guess what any of them were here for.

I walked over to Madison, who was sitting at a picnic table playing chess with another patient.

"Hi," I said, suddenly feeling self-conscious.

Madison whispered something to the kid she was playing with and walked over to me.

Mad looked the opposite of glamorous. But she also looked healthy.

I waited a second, afraid to hug her. But Mad wasn't at all hesitant. She put her long arms around me.

"You look good," I said over her shoulder.

Mad's model pout was replaced with a real genuine smile, the unguarded kind. The kind not meant for the camera. Her cheeks were pink—not from blush but from blushing.

"I feel enormous," she said when she pulled back from the hug. "But I know I'm not."

"How's it been?" I asked.

"It's hard. But I'll get there." She had focus in her eyes. I believed her.

"Enough about me," Mad said. "Tell me— how was it, supermodel?"

She led me to a tree in the courtyard outside and plopped down at the base of it. I kicked off the heels I was wearing and sat down beside her in the dirt.

I told her about everything. The show. Matt. Lorelei's offer.

When I finished, Mad leaned back against the tree. "It's not Lorelei's fault. It's the same everywhere. You should take the offer. It's a great one. And I'd love it if one of us could stay in the fashion world."

"What? You want to give it all up?"

"Well, not everything. I'm penning a column for *Teen Dream*. And my agent says that there's interest in my story for a movie of the week. I might even try acting. I know it comes with another set of issues—but I think I want to give it a shot. Look, modeling was never my dream. And you shouldn't give up yours."

I swallowed hard. Mad didn't want me getting weepy on her.

"So—chess, huh?"

"I always wanted to learn," Mad said. "And I have all this free time. And the kids here are all pretty cool. I could teach you sometime."

"I would love that. How about next weekend?"

She looked up, as if she was a little surprised I said yes.

As I walked back toward the lobby, I turned back to see Madison at play. She moved a piece across the board and said, "Your move."

* * *

As I walked out of the rehab center, my phone beeped. A text.

Matt: Our spot. One hour.

Me: I have to make a stop first.

When I got to Lorelei's office, she was sitting at her desk, pouring over reviews of the launch.

She looked up, not surprised to see me.

But suddenly I was surprised. On Lorelei's desk, next to her iPad, was the folder of Jamie's designs. Maybe change was possible. Maybe we just had to be brave enough to make it happen.

"I'll do it. But I have one condition," I said.

She laughed and leaned back in her chair to listen.

TWENTY-SEVEN

I was nervous. Matt and I hadn't talked since the runway. Since the kiss. I wondered if he'd changed his mind about me. I wonder if Lorelei had changed it for him.

This time, I got to our spot first. I sat on the grass and tucked my knees under my chin.

He sat next to me wordlessly, his expression unreadable. But his hand found mine.

"I know that Lorelei must hate me. I know she can make your life a nightmare. She could send you away."

"I don't care," he said. "Sure, I'd like you to

be here next summer. But we can find another way. There are other fashion houses in LA, and after the splash you made, you could write your own ticket. Maybe we could try New York."

We? I liked the sound of "we."

"Won't your mom have some kind of summer school plan for you next summer?"

"My plan is to be wherever you are," he said. "Besides if we tried New York, maybe I could take a few film classes."

I thought maybe Matt would have wanted me to do whatever it took to stay in the same city as him next summer. But instead, he wanted us both to be doing what we wanted.

"Film? That's so cool. But I don't think we have to go to New York. I think I'll meet you back here."

"Thea, are you sure . . . ?"

I nodded. "I think the only way I can change anything is from the inside out. Next season, if I stay, Lorelei says she'll use another model with a realistic body."

"Mom agreed to that?"

"She says she already thought of it. She

wants to do a model search every season with *Teen Dream*. It's great cross-promotion for the brand. And I know it doesn't change the world or anything. But whatever Lorelei Roy does, the rest of fashion follows."

"That's amazing. But I'm a little disappointed."

"Why?"

"I think you're a great model."

There was no pause after it. Nothing that meant, if only I was thinner. And I didn't make some joke about dieting forever. I was pretty sure that Lorelei's show was the last time I'd hit the runway as a model. But by the time I was a real designer, a girl who looked like me wouldn't be unthinkable. A girl like me might be the norm.

TWENTY-EIGHT

Dear Mr. Holt,

Last week, I walked down my first runway. Not in the way that I'd always dreamed, as a designer, but as a model wearing my own design. I never thought much about models. I'd even made jokes about them. But their place in the industry and in our culture is an important one. They aren't just walking clothes hangers. They're people with thoughts and feelings and problems. And I now count one of them as my friend. She made herself sick trying to live up to a perfect image. And I don't want other girls to do the same.

In fashion, they call the last dress in a show the showstopper. This summer, I was the showstopper—just one of the surprises of my incredible internship experience. I don't have any desire to model, but I think there should be a place for models that look something like me. I'm going to do everything I can to make a place for them while I make a place for myself in the business.

I was so excited about seeing the inside of a world I had always wanted to be a part of. I ended up seeing more than I had expected and doing more than I thought I was capable of. Thank you for the opportunity.

Sincerely,
Thea Roberts

ABOUT THE AUTHOR

D. M. Paige attended Columbia University and her first internship eventually led her to her first writing job at *Guiding Light*, a soap opera. She writes and lives in New York City

IT'S THE OPPORTUNITY OF A LIFETIME—
IF YOU CAN HANDLE IT.

Box Office Smash
D.M. PAIGE
THE OPPORTUNITY

The Campaign
ELIZABETH KARRE
THE OPPORTUNITY

Chart Topper
D.M. PAIGE
THE OPPORTUNITY

The Franchise
PATRICK JONES
with BRENT CHARTIER
THE OPPORTUNITY

Going to Press
D.M. PAIGE
THE OPPORTUNITY

Size 0
D.M. PAIGE
THE OPPORTUNITY

THE OPPORTUNITY